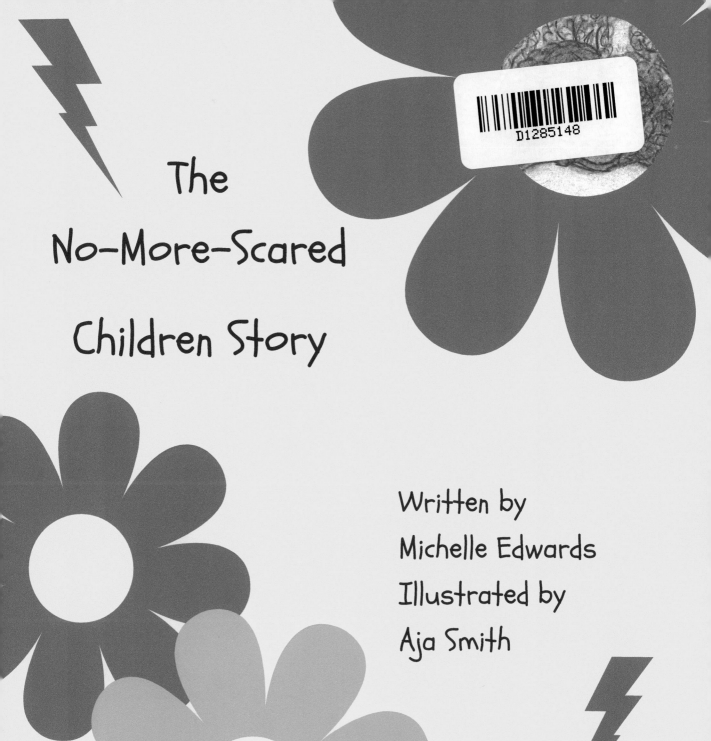

The No-More-Scared Children Story

Written by
Michelle Edwards
Illustrated by
Aja Smith

ISBN 978-1-63961-871-2 (paperback)
ISBN 978-1-68570-462-9 (hardcover)
ISBN 978-1-63961-872-9 (digital)

Christian Faith Publishing
832 Park Avenue
Meadville, PA 16335
www.christianfaithpublishing.com

Printed in the United States of America

To my children Morgen, Adam (April), and Grant who are told to reach for the stars and who push me to do the same.

Poem for Parents

God is mad. God is crying. God is so sad-all the things we are told or imply that we are bad. They say God is so angry and cannot hold His temper, so He yells from the sky to make us whimper. We are told raindrops that fall are tears from His eyes as He squeezes them shut shouting, "Oh, you guys!" Lightning flashes and crackles through the sky, making some jump and making some cry.

They say God is shaking His finger at us when there are little flashes, but He's pounding His fist when lightning crashes. Stomping His feet and waving hands wildly is the picture we get when winds aren't moving mildly. As little children we think the storm is coming from a monster, not from a God who is an awesome wonder.

As adults we watch the storm clouds gather—our minds reverting back to the mad God matter. We don't give it much thought, but the thought is still there that the monster in the sky is blowing about our air. As grown-ups we have never stopped and wondered—believing in such a monster is never really pondered. We know the grass grows, and the flowers bloom. We cut and clean them to decorate our rooms.

The trees bud and change to brilliant colors in the fall, prompting us to travel to see the beauty of it all. Why do we never think of God's laughter as thunder, of Him laughing and clapping at our numerous blunders? How about thinking of the lightning crisscrossing the sky as a vivid picture of His smile saying, "Hi."

Why not see the water from the sky as tears of laughter, bringing beauty to life on the day after. Try giving God the creator of the universe and air a good thought or word—it's only fair. No more scary God stories about a storm. Speaking of God's wonder, let that be our norm. Tell our children no more of monsters in the skies, only of the beauty God creates for our eyes.

Come on Keisha, come out Darvon
let's get outside, let's get gone.
God is showing out without the sun,
so let's get out there and have some fun.

Our parents decided to change the mad God story
so out we go with little worry.
The sky is dark and scary and gray,
but outside we'll stay to sing and play.

The thunder in our ears like a mighty roar,
makes us jump and giggle all the more.
We get a little nervous when the lightning flashes,
so we pause what we are doing until it passes.

The wind in our face is like a grandma's kiss
when she grabs to hug us—her eyes all a mist.
Lightning done and thunder at low pitch,
we laugh so hard we get a stitch.

It keeps storming and the raindrops keep falling
not one of us is scared—not one of us bawling.
Jumping from puddle to puddle as we go,
without getting covered in mud head to toe.

We are no longer scared of the monster in the sky.
The rain is God's way of calling us outside.
Knowing God is not mad we go out in a hurry.
Thank you parents for changing the mad God story.

About the Author

Michelle Edwards was born in Texas but grew up in Iowa. She has three adult children and four wonderful grandchildren. Michelle loves reading, writing, music, transforming trash to treasures, and having fun with family and friends. Her love of reading and writing, and the encouragement from other's led her to write this book. She has also co-written a song.

Her faith is very important to her and it has helped her conquer many fears, one of those being the fear of storms. Having survived a tornado and derecho, she knows what bad weather is. By writing this book she hopes that when the rain starts to fall it will become a little less frightening for her readers and brings a smile to their faces.

The No-More-Scared Children Story is Michelle's first book.

About the Illustrator

Aja Smith was born and raised in Des Moines, Iowa. She is a 2021 graduate of the Des Moines public school system and the Central and Virtual Academy. She received academic honors overcoming the roadblocks of being diagnosed with autism.

Aja's creative pursuits add to her list of accomplishments. She wrote a TV pilot script and received first place in the Jr. High Magazine's 6 Feet 6 Weeks National Short Film Contest. The short film aired in Los Angeles, California, in 2020.

When asked if she would use her gifts to illustrate my book, *The No-More-Scared Children Story*, she said, "Yes!"

Acknowledgments

Thank you, God.

Thank you to Aja Smith, who made my book come alive.

Thank you to Paula, Sarah, Kim S., Kim F., and Marcy who continually show me that you are the change in your own life.

Thank you to Amy at Copyworks for making this project a reality.

CPSIA information can be obtained
at www.ICGtesting.com
Printed in the USA
BVHW022300250822
645564BV00005B/69